The Summer Night

Newly illustrated edition

by Charlotte Zolotow   pictures by Ben Shecter

HarperCollins*Publishers*

The Summer Night
Text copyright © 1958, 1974 by Charlotte Zolotow
Illustrations copyright © 1974, 1991 by Ben Shecter
Printed in the U.S.A. All rights reserved.
1   2   3   4   5   6   7   8   9   10
Newly illustrated edition

Library of Congress Cataloging-in-Publication Data
Zolotow, Charlotte, date
    The summer night / by Charlotte Zolotow ; pictures by Ben Shecter.
        p.   cm.
    Summary: After she and her father take a walk and have a bedtime
snack, a little girl is finally sleepy enough to go to bed.
    ISBN 0-06-026916-2. — ISBN 0-06-026917-0 (lib. bdg.)
    1. Bedtime—Fiction. [1. Sleep—Fiction.] I. Shecter, Ben,
ill. II. Title.
PZ7.Z77Sv   1991   88-44522
[E]—dc20   CIP
                                                                    AC

For my father

Louis J. Shapiro

The little girl's father

took care of her all day.

In the evening he bathed her

and put her to bed.

But the little girl wasn't sleepy.

"I'm thirsty," she said.

He brought her a cup of water.

"I'm hungry," she said.

Her father brought her an apple.

"I'm hot," she said.

Her father opened the window

and the soft night air came in.

She looked out into the darkness.

The sky was full of stars.

The little girl's eyes were

bright as the stars,

and her father could understand

why on this soft summer night

she wasn't sleepy.

So he took her up in his arms
and carried her down the stairs.
Only one lamp was on in the
living room, but the moonlight shone
in through the big window,
making everything in the room
a new shape and size.
The gold clock on the mantelpiece
seemed to say,

night-time

night-time

night-time

"Read me a story,"
the little girl said.
Her father read her
a long story in his
slow deep voice,
but when he closed the book,
her eyes were still bright,
and he knew she
wasn't sleepy yet.

He sat down

on the piano bench

and the little girl

leaned against him

and he played some

soft nighttime music,

so gently the sounds hung

like little birds in the air,

warm and feathery and sweet.

But when her father

finished the song

the little girl still

wasn't sleepy.

"We'll go for a walk," her father said.
The little girl slipped her hand in his.
The screen door closed behind them
like a whisper in the night.
Far away a train whistle sounded.
The little girl moved closer to her
father as they started toward
the backyard path.
Lightning bugs like little darts
of fire led the way.

They came to the pond.

It looked like a pool

of black shiny ink.

At the water's edge

two rabbits stopped still

and stared at them

before they bounded

into the bushes

and were gone.

The father
and little girl
sat by the pond.
On the opposite bank
a family of white ducks
were sleeping
with their heads pillowed
in their own soft feathers.
The moon,
reflected in the pond,
seemed so close
the little girl felt
she could reach
into the water
and hold the moon
in her hands.

The lilacs from the house
smelled sweet and stronger
than they did in the daytime.
"Mmmmmmmmm,"
said the little girl,
leaning against her father.
"Watch," he said.
He threw a pebble
into the smooth pond.
They watched the circles
rippling out and out
in the black water
while the splash of the stone
echoed in the stillness
of the night.

"Now, let's go,"
the father said at last,
holding out his hand.
The little girl
put hers
in his and they started
back to the house.
The lighted kitchen window
shone through the darkness.
Near the house they heard
a little bell tinkling.
It was the bell their cat wore
to warn the birds away.

Whooooooooooo

Whoooooooooooooooooooo

WHOOOOOooooooooooooooooo

A long sound came

from the owl in the tree

behind the house

as the father

opened the screen door.

He sat the little girl

at the kitchen table

and they had warm milk

and bread and butter

with brown sugar.

Now the father saw

that the little girl's eyes

were dreamy and sleepy at last.

So he carried her upstairs

and put her to bed again.

He bent down to kiss her

and the little girl kissed him back.

Outside the night owl cried again.

Whooooooooooo

Whooooooooooooooooooooo

WHOOOOOoooooooooooooooooo

But this time the little girl didn't hear.

She was fast asleep.

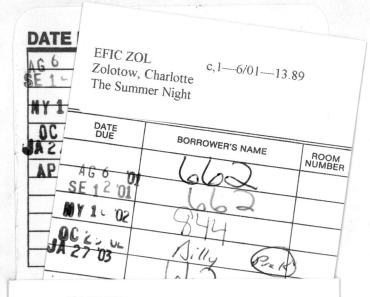

EFIC ZOL c,1—6/01—13.89
Zolotow, Charlotte
The Summer Night

DATE DUE	BORROWER'S NAME	ROOM NUMBER
AG 6 '01	662	
SE 1 2 '01	662	
MY 1 '02	844	
OC 2 '02		
JA 27 03	Billy	(P₂R)

EFIC ZOL c,1—6/01—13.89
Zolotow, Charlotte
The Summer Night